DC DEAR SUPER-VILLAINS

Written by
Michael Northrop

Illustrated by
Gustavo Duarte

Colored by
Cris Peter

Lettered by
Wes Abbott

SUPERMAN created by Jerry Siegel and Joe Shuster.
By special arrangement with the Jerry Siegel family.

SARA MILLER Editor
STEVE COOK Design Director - Books
AMIE BROCKWAY-METCALF Publication Design

MARIE JAVINS Editor-in-Chief, DC Comics
MICHELE R. WELLS VP & Executive Editor, Young Reader

DANIEL CHERRY III Senior VP - General Manager
JIM LEE Publisher & Chief Creative Officer
DON FALLETTI VP - Manufacturing Operations & Workflow Management
LAWRENCE GANEM VP - Talent Services
ALISON GILL Senior VP - Manufacturing & Operations
NICK J. NAPOLITANO VP - Manufacturing Administration & Design
NANCY SPEARS VP - Revenue

DEAR DC SUPER-VILLAINS

DC Comics, 2900 West Alameda Ave., Burbank, CA 91505

Printed by LSC Communications, Crawfordsville, IN, USA. 2/26/21.

First Printing.

ISBN: 978-1-77950-054-0

PEFC Certified
This product is from sustainably managed forests and controlled sources
PEFC
PEFC/29-31-337
www.pefc.org

Library of Congress Cataloging-in-Publication Data
Names: Northrop, Michael, writer. | Duarte, Gustavo, 1977- illustrator. | Peter, Cris, colourist. | Abbott, Wes, letterer.
Title: Dear DC Super-Villains : a graphic novel / written by Michael Northrop ; illustrated by Gustavo Duarte ; colored by Cris Peter ; lettered by Wes Abbott.
Description: Burbank, CA : DC Comics, [2021] | "Superman created by Jerry Siegel and Joe Shuster. By special arrangement with the Jerry Siegel family." | Audience: Ages 8-12 | Audience: Grades 4-6 | Summary: "Peek inside the lives of DC's infamous rogues gallery, where curious kids write to notorious scoundrels, asking them about life on the dark side. Read between the lines and you may notice the baddies are up to something big! Will the Justice League show up in time to stop them?"-- Provided by publisher.
Identifiers: LCCN 2020049440 | ISBN 9781779500540 (trade paperback)
Subjects: LCSH: Graphic novels. | CYAC: Graphic novels. | Supervillians--Fiction. | Superheroes--Fiction.
Classification: LCC PZ7.7.N678 Des 2021 | DDC 741.5/973--dc23

TABLE OF CONTENTS

CHAPTER 1

Dear Catwoman

Cairo, Egypt.
The hour is late, the moon is full, and the museum is filled with priceless treasure.

It is a time for dark deeds. A time for those who avoid the spotlight.

It is a time, in a word, for villains.
KLIK! KLIK!
And this one is purrfect for the job.

Her name is
Selina Kyle.
She is fierce.
Female.
Feline.
But you can call her...
Dear
Catwoman

And like a cat,
she always lands
on her feet.

Faaaa-

Whiiiip!

If she
lands
at all.
Lasers.
Sneaky.

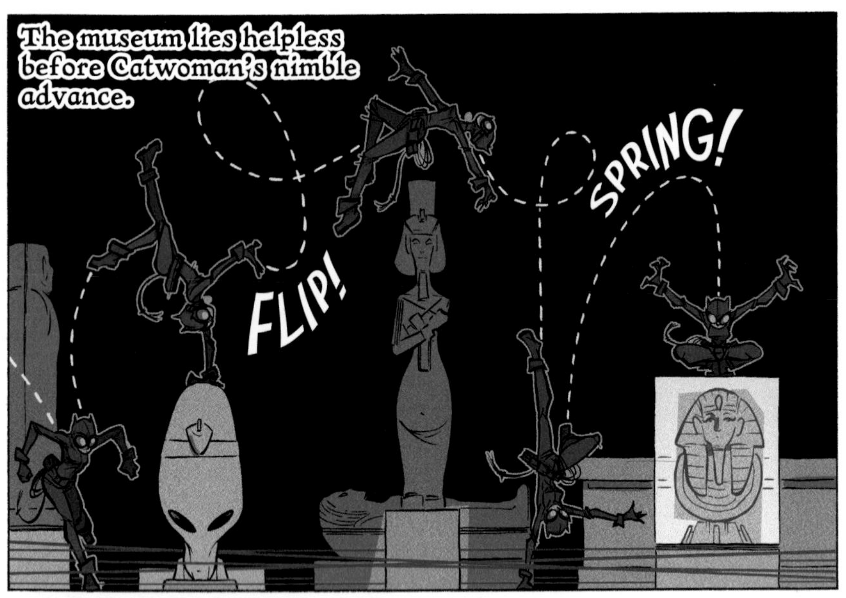
The museum lies helpless before Catwoman's nimble advance.
FLIP!
SPRING!

And she doesn't plan on leaving empty-handed.

FLOP!
LOOT SACK!

No item is safe.
Especially if it's shiny.
GLEAM!

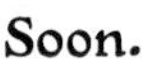
Soon.

Clink! Clonk!
This thing is heavy.
Don't know how Santa does it.

Also soon.
SHREEE-TEE-SHREEE!
TONE DEAF!

But then...

SHREEE-TEE-SHREEE!
SENSITIVE CAT EARS!
Uh-oh! Better pounce!

Gold cat statuette.
1500 B.C.
Value:
$10 million.
Soooo pretty.

Stop! Thief!
KRSHT
Cat burglar in main gallery!

The early bird gets the worm...
But does the greedy cat get tazed?!
BRRZZZ!

Nope!
ZZZAPP!
Tazed my bag, bro!

TOO SLOW!
CATNIP

Heh heh.

The rooftops of Cairo.
RUNNING FREE!

Later.
Bejeweled and chillin' on her phone.
clik-clik
To: The Legion of Doom Tip Line of Evil
Attention: Catwoman
Dear Catwoman,
You have all the agility and instincts of a fierce wild cat.
Batman has no powers at all.
How does he ever beat you?
Curiously yours,
Kat C.

Five thousand six hundred miles from Gotham and they still ask me about that Bat.
Still... this little Kat might have a point. How does he do it?
Her mind wanders back...
Memory.
All alone in the moonlight.

Gotham
Oh, look, the Dim Knight.
It's all over, Catwoman!
Things always start well for me...

And it's not like his attacks are anything to flip over...
BATARANG!
Fa-Lip!

And he's always such a regular guy around me...
Errk?
Yoink!
So...down to earth.

True, he never stays down for long.
BUH-BOOT!

MUH-MISS!
BAT-BUTT!

This Bat-Glue-Bomb will slow you down!

POW!
Nope!

His tricks never stick. So how does he stop me?
You're out of moves, Bat-Bumbler.
Well, there is one more thing...

BAT-LASER-POINTER!
CAT BRAIN: ON
HUMAN BRAIN: OFF
My memory always gets a little fuzzy at the end.

Back in Egypt.
How does he ever beat you?

TYPITY TYPE TYPE

New message from Catwoman

Little Kat,
Who can say?
The Bat works in mysterious ways.
Purrfectly yours,
CW
P.S. Don't wo

The guards burst onto the roof!

Too slow. Again.

P.S. Don't worry about me, precious thing. We villains don't tend to stay caught for long.

CHAPTER 2

Dear Lex Luthor

LL197

Blackgate Penitentiary.
A formidable fortress rising from the cold and churning waters of Gotham Bay.
This is a place for villains, too.
At least the ones who got caught...

Lex Luthor~criminal mastermind and Superman's greatest foe~still can't believe he's one of them.
Ya got some mail today, Luthor.
Waste of postage if ya ask me.
flip!
I didn't.
Letters for Lex.

YOU CAN'T KEEP ME IN THIS DEPLORABLE PLACE!

I AM THE GREATEST CRIMINAL MIND OF ALL TIME!

Or at least the baldest!

Lex Luthor's Wall of Fame.
(Or shame, depending on who you ask.)

LEX LASHES OUT WITH LATEST LASER!

Daily Planet
LUTHOR UNLEASHES CRIME WAVE!

BUSINESS INVESTOR DAILY
ALL RIGHT, WHO KEEPS SELLING THIS GUY KRYPTONITE?

LUTHOR'S ROBOT SENDS SUPERMAN FLYING!

LEX LUTHOR: TOO SMART FOR OUR OWN GOOD

BAD GUYS WEEKLY
VILLAIN OF THE YEAR: IT'S LEX—AGAIN!

LUTHOR ZAPS THE MAN OF STEEL

THE NATIONAL WORRIER
CAN ANYONE STOP LUTHOR?

The reviews are in.

Lex Luthor is one bad dude.

A criminal genius of epic proportions.

LUTHOR LOCKED UP!

But even geniuses make mistakes.

So write now.
Because right now,
he's got time on his hands.

And, at least for the moment,
we know where to find him.

Dear Lex Luthor

To: Lex Luthor
Blackgate Penitentiary
Wobegone Island
Gotham Bay
At least the children can appreciate my towering intellect!
Yo Luthor!
I heard you're a criminal genius. What's so brilliant about getting caught? Maybe we should call you Lex Loser!
Not sincerely,
Joe Mama
LL1979

Okay, maybe not *this* kid.
Little punk.
Rip!
Tear!
Rip!

Hmmm.
LL1979

The “fan mail” isn’t going so great today, but Lex opens the next one anyway.

He’s an optimist at heart.

You don’t make a career of fighting Superman if you’re not.

RRRRRiiiiiP!

Dear Lex,

If you're so smart, why haven't you cured baldness?

Peace out,
Billy Bosu

Finally, a letter I can answer.
My public needs me!
LL 1979

Dear Billy,
Who says I haven't cured baldness?

I called it Lex-gaine.

FIZZLE-POP

DA-RRIP!

I was so excited, I decided to test it on myself.

RUB-A-RUB

Then I waited.

SKRITCH SKRITCH

Were my days as a ping-pong ball finally over?

It was a hair-raising experience.

But then...

You've done it again, Lex, you handsome devil!

Yoinks!
Darn that itchy nose.

Remember, Billy. Always wash your hands after experiments.

The next day.
I set out to cure baldness...
And things got hairy.
PSSHHOOOSH!

I guess you could say it was a close shave.
Not my greatest invention, but it taught me an important lesson.

GLEAM!
Bald is beautiful!

The other thing it taught me...
dribble-
dribble

The bathroom sink shares a pipe with the shower.

AAAAH!

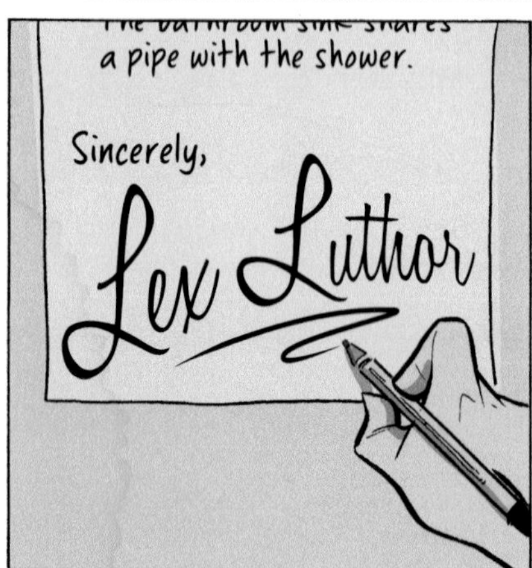
a pipe with the shower.
Sincerely,
Lex Luthor

P.S. Tell no one. Or I will find you.
LL1979

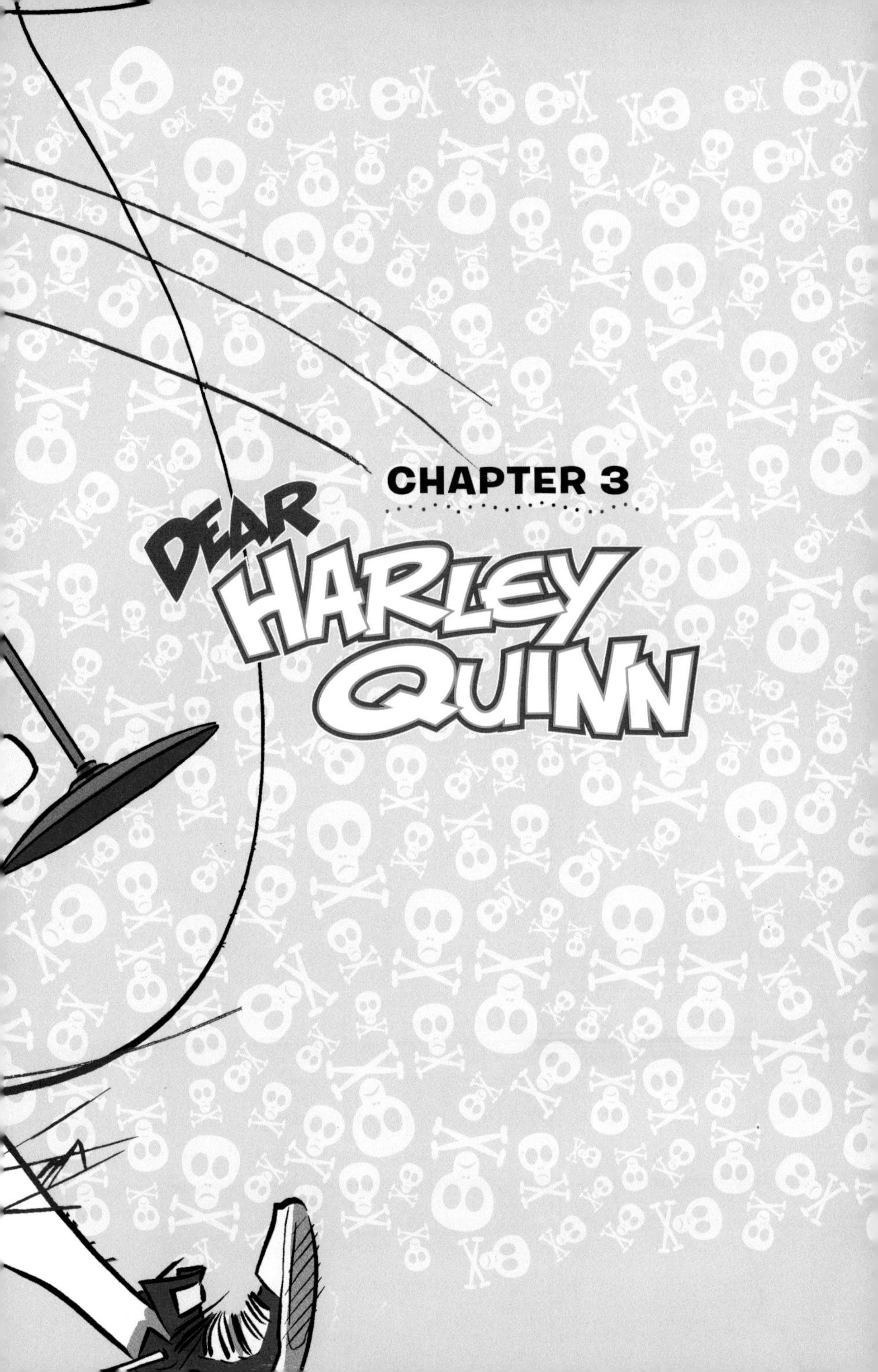
CHAPTER 3
DEAR HARLEY QUINN

She is chaos in human form, trouble walking on two legs. Her real name is Harleen Quinzel, but no one calls her that.
Instead, she goes by Harley Quinn. And the only thing you ever know for sure about her is that you never know what she'll do next.
DEAR HARLEY QUINN

After a long day of turning Gotham City upside down, she's kicking back at the Hall of Doom— home to the world's fiercest villains...

TIP TAP TIP TAP
And answering texts from fans, foes, and kids who are just curious about a girl who is so *good* at being *bad*.

Dear Harley,
You seem super funny! If this super-villain thing doesn't work out, have you considered a career in stand-up comedy?
LOL,
Maria Rio

Hey, Maria! It's funny you mention it. I gave comedy a try once...

GOTHAM
LAF SHAK
Give it up for your next comedian here at open mic night...
Harrrrrley Quinnnnnnn!

Come on, Harls. You got this.
GOTHAM
HIGH
LOW

Hey, Gotham!
More like Got-HAM, am I right?

Chirp
Chirp
ACTUAL CRICKET!
ZZZZZZZ

Okay... here's a joke for you.
shuffle shuffle
Why didn't— nah, wait... I mean...

ahem

CHICKEN CROSSING ROAD JOKES

GOLD!

CÓ!

WHY DID THE CHICKEN CROSS

tap tap

Why'd the chicken cross the—

To get away from your terrible jokes! ***Hee hee!***

HAHAHAHAHAHAHAHAHAHA!
Lucky chicken!

Guess I'm the only *real* Joker here.

Okay, mister.
I got a punchline for ya...

WUH-BAM!
YAAAH!
Not funny!

TAP TIP TIP
So, yeah, I tried comedy. I was a big ***hit.***
Not sure it's for me, though. I'm not great with…criticism.

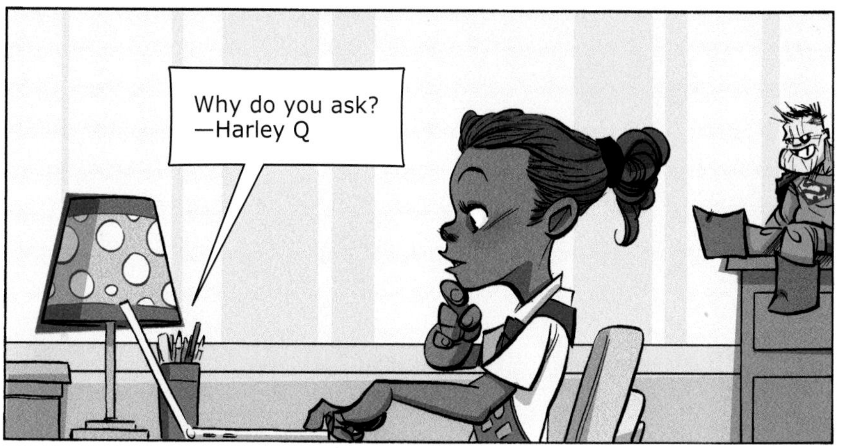
Why do you ask?
—Harley Q

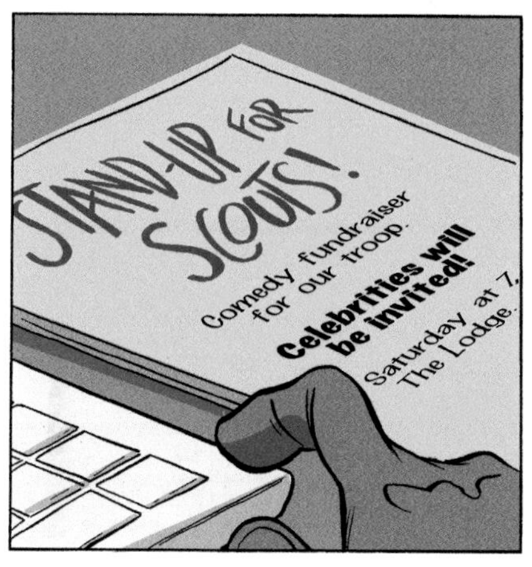
STAND-UP FOR SCOUTS!
Comedy fundraiser for our troop.
Celebrities will be invited!
Saturday at 7, The Lodge.

No reason!
Can I interest you in some cookies?
TAPPITY
TAP TAP TAP

Kid,
I'm ***always*** interested in cookies.
BOOP!
Auto alert:
Daily meeting
Starting: 5 minutes ago
SNOOZE AGAIN?
KA-FLIP!
Gotta go!
TYPITY TIP TAP TYPE

Some hallways are filled with music. Some are silent.
SMACK-O!

The soundtrack of the Hall of Doom...
Let go! It's my turn to use the death ray!
POP!
...is arguments.

Says who? Give it here!
Never!
GRAB! TUSSLE!
So many arguments.

Whoopsie.
ZAARP!

Oh great. You killed the last plant.
I killed it? You're the one with baseball mitts for hands!
plurp!
KITCHEN
of DOOM!

I know you took my bananas, Sinestro!
WHUMP!
My coffee— AIYEE!

I told you, fuzzball. If it's yellow, it's mine!
grumble, grumble

Gack!
P-U!

Do it again and I'll shove that power ring right up your—
SLAM!
MILK

That milk expired a month ago.
GLUG-GLUG-GLUG
MILK

Now it's yogurt.
CHEW-CHEW
MILK

Anyway, see you guys in there.

BURRRP!
PA-DUMP!
MILK

See us in where?

Hey, bladey lady.
Aren't we supposed to have a meeting now?
EXTRA BUTT-ROOM
HAIR
ALGAE
FORMER BUBBLE
HARLEY QUINN
BLACK MANTA
GRODD
Rrumble!

GLEAM!
LEX LUTHOR, CEO
CHIEF EVIL OFFICER
mew?
CATWOMAN
NOT A-PEELING
SINESTRO
Ten minutes ago.
KATANA

CHAPTER 4

DEAR GORILLA GRODD

You might be thinking:
A big ape.
Strong.
Dumb.
You're half right.
He's as strong as a freight train.
But he's smart, too.
A genius.
And his superpowers?
They're mental.
Mind control and more.
So change your mind now...
Or he'll change it for you!
DEAR GORILLA GRODD

Grodd's room.
KLIK!
No humans allowed.

Fancy place.
Sophisticated.

Sinestro makes me so mad.
Perhaps some chess to soothe the nerves...

Thirty seconds later...
1
Grandmaster Grodd wins again.

BOOOP!
What now?

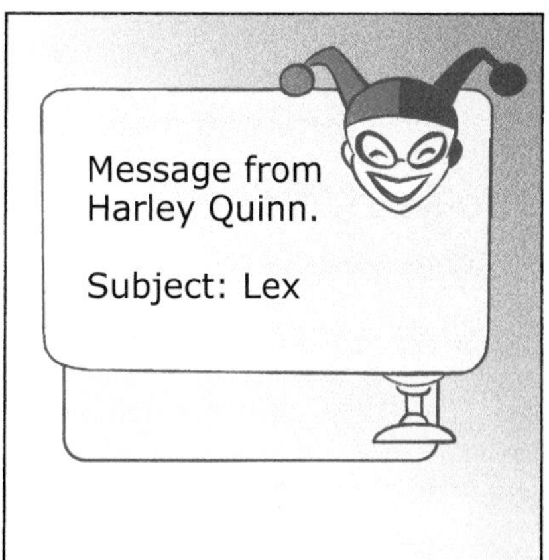
Message from Harley Quinn.
Subject: Lex

Lex, Lex, Lex.
What's the big deal? I'm just as smart as him—but no one wants to take orders from an ape.
Maybe I can find something worth my time on the tip line.
KLICK!
DELETE!

LEGION OF DOOM
TIP LINE OF EVIL

New messages:

To Lex Luthor...
To Katana...
To Lex Luthor...
To Harley Quinn...
To Lex Luthor...
To Sinestro...
To Lex Luthor...
To Giganta...
To Lex Luthor...

SCROLL... SCROLL...

To that monkey dude...
Grumble grumble

"That monkey dude"?
Monkeys have tails...
I'm an ape!
TAIL-FREE ZONE!

I'll set this human straight.
KA-LICK!

Dear Madd Monkey or whatever,

I'm having trouble learning my multiplication tables. The first five aren't so bad, but after that... Anyway, my friend says that if the Legion of Doom has a monkey who can build space lasers, I ought to be able to figure out six times seven. So my question: How'd you get so smart?

Counting on your reply,
Hunter Thomas

Dear juvenile human,
First of all, gorillas are apes. Great apes, in fact, just like humans. And like a human—well, ***some*** humans—I've always been smart. All the gorillas in Gorilla City are. And okay, sure, maybe I wasn't always the best student but...
SMACKETY-SMACK!

Blah blah math. *Blah blah* homework.

YOUNG GRODD!

It was last period. A.P. calculus.

They say the *A.P.* stands for "advanced placement."

I say it's "ape punishment."

The point is, I was bored.
Staring out the window (as usual).
Dreaming of adventures beyond those stifling school walls.
!
That's when I saw it.
There were two options.
Either I'd fallen asleep in class again and was dreaming...
Or that was a meteor.
RED-HOT SPACE ROCK!
FIERY TRAIL!
(What? I paid attention *sometimes*.)
Finally, something cool!
I watched closely to see where it would land.
Who can tell me the answer? Grodd? Grodd?

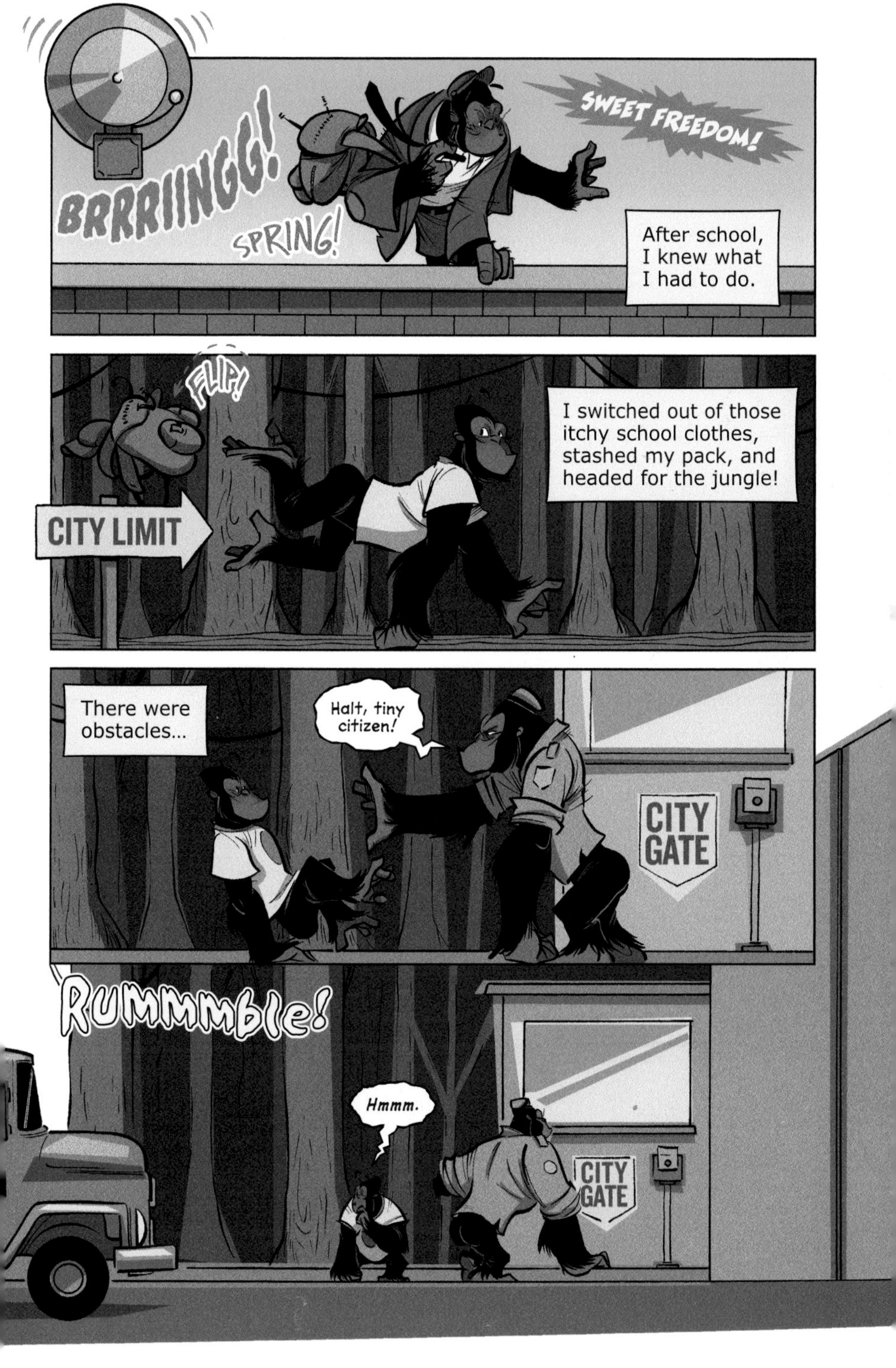

BRRRIINGG!
SPRING!
SWEET FREEDOM!
After school, I knew what I had to do.

FLIP!
CITY LIMIT
I switched out of those itchy school clothes, stashed my pack, and headed for the jungle!

There were obstacles...

Halt, tiny citizen!

CITY GATE

RUMMMBLE!

Hmmm.

CITY GATE

But nothing insurmountable.

I just rolled with it.
tumble,
tumble
Oof!
VROOM SPUTTER VROOM

I was in the jungle.

Right where I wanted to be.

EEEEET!

EEEEET!

Be careful what you wish for.

ROAR!

HIIISSSS!

It was a big jungle.

And I was a little ape.

[=one million acres]

[=so smol!]

Was I scared?

Please.

GRAB!

I had a meteor to find!

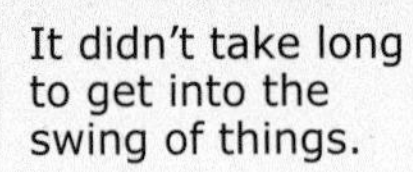
It didn't take long to get into the swing of things.

METEOR QUEST!

A-ha!

HIIIISSSSS!
The search wasn't easy.
TIGHT SQUEEZE!

But I tied things up quickly.
YOINKS!

Eureka!

I was amazed.
This rock had traveled countless miles and landed at my feet.
I crept closer...

Too close.

ARRGH!

Vapors... changing... my... brain!

ALIEN UPGRADE!

RRRIPP!

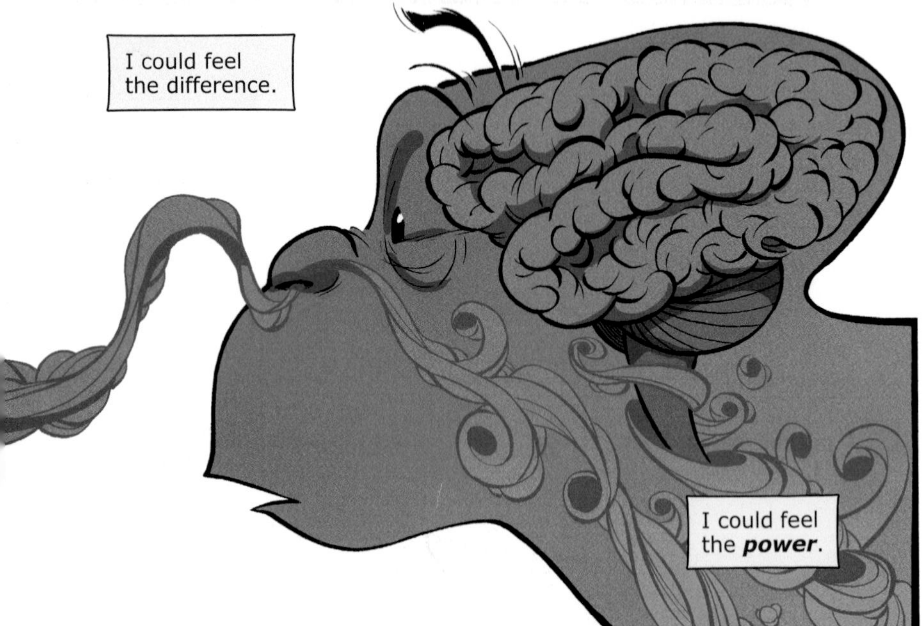

I could feel the difference.

I could feel the ***power***.

The jungle was still a dangerous place...

But not for me.
MIND CONTROL!

I struggled to comprehend the changes, to contain the energy.

But then I realized...
TELEKINESIS!
TREE-MENDOUS!

Why contain such power?
Whoa.

You again?

You're in big tr—

Grrik!
I could get used to this.

And I **have** gotten used to it.
BANANA SPLIT!

So you see, Hunter—hate that name, BTW—I earned this brainpower. Everyone in that classroom was smart. But I was curious.
That's what set me apart. Multiplying six times seven isn't about adding six seven times...

It's about wondering how math works. Once you understand the system, there's always a shortcut...
42!

You just need to stay curious!
SEND!
PLICK!

What's this, a postscript?
P.S. Could you pass this on to Lex when you're done? No offense, but I need an A.

Grrrrr...
Stay curious— just like I'm curious what the Legion could do with some fresh leadership.

CHAPTER 5

DEAR GIGANTA

Dangerous cargo rolls down a city street.
And its owner, a global weapons manufacturer, is taking no chances.
TALON CORP

Bulletproof cars and armed guards.
A truck with armor a foot thick.
Inside, the infamous cablumium molecule.

Big precautions for a big prize.
BOOMP!
Whoa!
What was that?
KRONK!
But the threat is even bigger.

Dr. Doris Zuel.
Talk about girl power.
She's smart, strong, ruthless.
She's not always this big...
But she *grows* on you.
Oh dear...
DEAR GIGANTA
SKA-REECH!

HAWNK!

TALON CORP

BA-DOOM...

BA-DOOM...

Open the gate, or I'll peel the place like a grape!
SHOOOOP!

Gettin' low...
SHRINKING!
Low...
Low!

Stone-cold shorty.

Wish this thing looked less like a big mouth.

Did you just steal that because it's shiny?
I'm a **scientist,** Sinestro.
Not my question.

I don't **hate** that it's shiny.

Oops!
BOMP!
Hey, watch it!

Should've known it was you, bigfoot.
Sorry, Harley.
What's the **big** rush, anyway?

You never answered my message, Grodd, ya big ape.
We're gonna need your muscle tomorrow—so don't **FUR**-get!
HEE-HEE.

That's all we are to them: muscle.
And *big* jokes.
How could I **FUR**-get?

You've got a message on the tip line.
Thanks, big guy.
GIGANTA'S ROOM:
KEEP BACK 50 FEET

What a day!

WHOOMP!

Tablet? Phone? There's not much difference at six feet, six inches.
PLINK!

To: The Legion of Doom Tip Line of Evil

Attention: Giganta

Dear Giganta,

I know you're big trouble—like, really big trouble—but I can kind of see where you're coming from. I'm the tallest girl in my class, and it's not always easy...

Class photo...

BEHEADED!

School play...

THAT'S SOME ELF!

Respect your elf— and yourself!

Field trip...

WHAP!
BRANCHING OUT!

It's not easy standing out—or up—and sometimes the other kids make fun of me. Any tips would be appreciated. The problem seems to be, well, growing.
Sincerely,
Lexi Lolo
P.S. I swear these aren't tall tales.

TAP TIP TAP
Hey Lexi,
I hear ya, sister. People can be jerks when you're different. I learned that lesson early too. But I learned something else. What makes us different makes us special. Sometimes it's not so bad to rise above the crowd...

For example, it's always tablet time when you can reach the hiding spot!
Gimme!

And there are major advantages...
Mittens!
That'll be five bucks, Toby.

...to rising above the competition!
MONSTER JAM!
POSTERIZED!

Message from Harley Quinn.

Subject: GIANT mission tomorrow!

Anyway, got to get some rest. Just learned I have a big day coming up. A ***very*** big day.

Stand tall,
Giganta

Can't grab it, can't have it!
Heh heh!
Give it back!
BIZARRO

PLUCK!
What the—?
BIZARRO

My Twinkies!
Bon appétit, little buddy.
BIZARRO

CHAPTER 6

Dear Sinestro

There is an energy that runs through the universe: the emotional electromagnetic spectrum.

White: Life
Green: WillpoWer
Red: RAGE
Blue: HOPE
Orange: GREED
Indigo: Compassion
Yellow: FEAR
Violet: Love
Black: Death

The Red Lantern Atrocitus harnesses the raw power of rage.
BEEEZ!
The hero Green Lantern uses willpower to give form to his emerald creations.
CHUG-A-CHUG-A

And the Yellow Lantern known as Sinestro?

He uses *fear.*
For the one who instills fear wields great power.
And no one wields it better than Thaal Sinestro. Bane of planet Korugar. Arch-nemesis of Green Lantern.
And right now, he is a man on a mission, so...
GET OUT OF THE WAY!
SQUA-SQUAWK!
FEAR ~~Dear~~ Sinestro!

Hum, what to ask?

Dear Sinestro...

Dear Sinestro,

Are you always so mean?
Wouldn't it be nicer to be...nicer?

Just curious,
Ann Onni-Muss

A message? Now?
Better not check it while I'm flying.
Could crash into a building or something.
BOOP!

It's probably just one of my annoying coworkers, anyway.
Space...
OUT OF THIS WORLD!

Besides, I've got bigger things to worry about.
Once I steal the top secret Mega-Laser from this space station, everyone will fear my name!

What's this?

Atrocitus!
He must be after the Mega-Laser, too.
And he's moving fast!

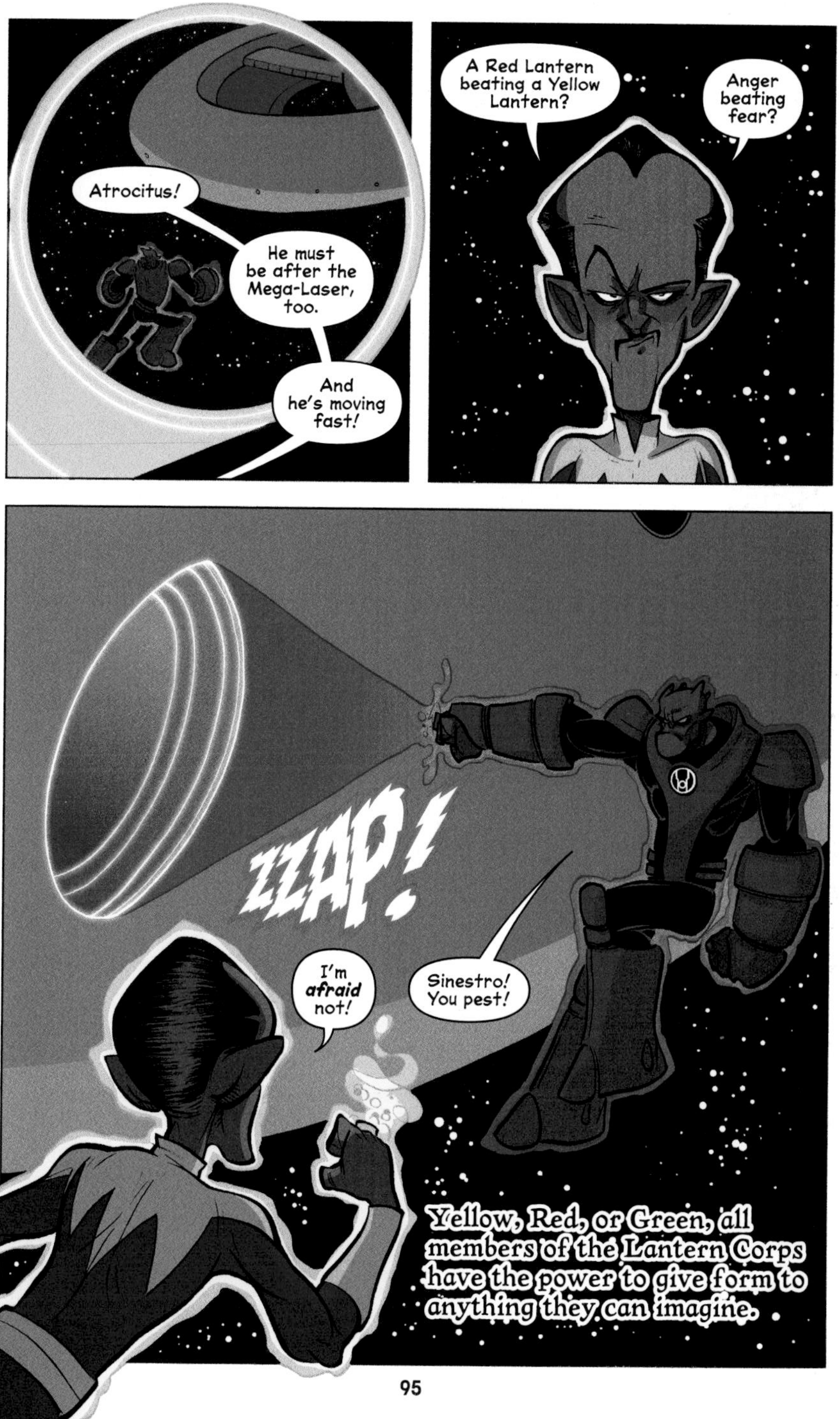

A Red Lantern beating a Yellow Lantern?
Anger beating fear?

ZZAP!

Sinestro! You pest!

I'm *afraid* not!

Yellow, Red, or Green, all members of the Lantern Corps have the power to give form to anything they can imagine.

GARK!
THOMP!
You've been book clubbed!
Their fights always start out very creatively.

AWWF!
Since you're so well red...
SLAM!

But after a while...
Better duck!
QUACK!
The ideas run thin.

But just as the battle is about to get corny...
Shucks!

A flash of YELLOW!

Myooo?

A kitten!
So soft, so cute, so... yellow.

I will call her...
SUNBEAM!

KA-BLAMMO!

Sunbeam, sweet thing...

My mother never let me have a pet.
But you could be that pet...

And rule beside me in terror!
MREOW?

But Atrocitus is fueled by the power of rage!
I can show no weakness—and you are so vulnerable.

I must lead him away to keep you safe.
Farewell, precious Sunbeam!
Hull failure!
Space suits, everyone!

Later. Nearly home.
sniffle
Oh yes, I'd forgotten. My message.
BOOP!

Am I always so mean?

Pull it together, Yellow Lantern.
You have a reputation to uphold!
SWH-LAP!

Dear misguided child,
Yes, always very mean.

Sinisterly,
Sinestro

SEND!

Meanwhile...
Meow?
BEST FRIENDS FURREVER!
MEGA -LASER-
MEW!

CHAPTER 7

Dear Katana

Dear Katana
Tatsu Yamashiro.
A samurai without
a master.
A warrior for hire.
Sometimes she's
hired to do good.
Sometimes she's
hired to do *bad.*
Right now, she's
only out for herself.
She does what she wants.
She takes what she needs.
And right now...

...she needs a Band-Aid.
Can't believe I dropped my sword.
Again.
I'm really off my game lately.

桜
OUCHIE-AIDS
Pipto
GUMMIES
Let's see...vitamins: no. Floss: ***Definitely*** not.
Ah, there you are.

OUCHIE-AIDS
FLICK!

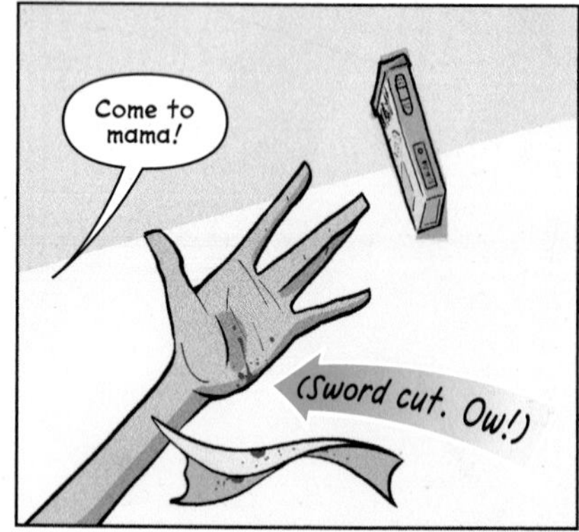

Come to mama!
(Sword cut. Ow!)

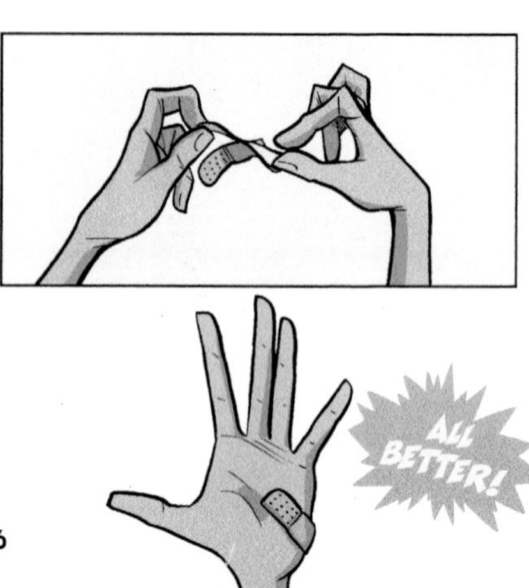

ALL BETTER!

Minutes later, in the Elevator of Doom.
Bay-bee shark, doo-doo...
ELEVATOR MUSIC OF DOOM!

Top floor: swamp views and assorted villains.
BING!

Have you been *crying?*
No.
Shut up.

I see you're returning from your "top secret" mission empty-handed.
Emptier than you'll ever know.
Snnorrt!

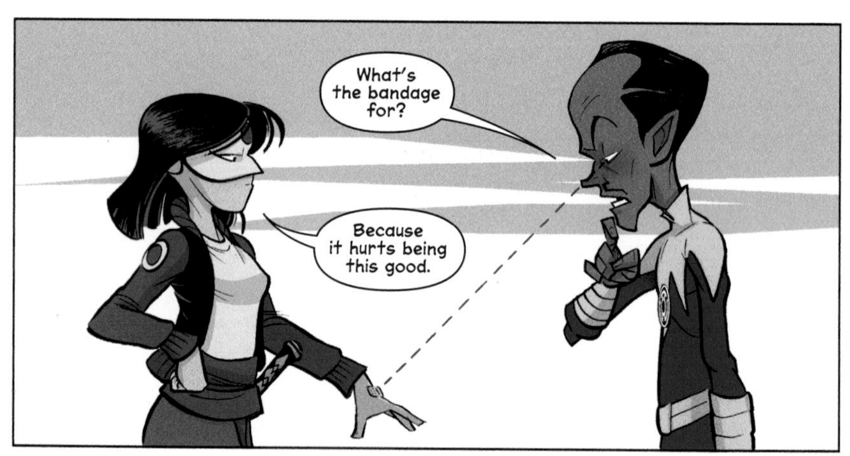
What's the bandage for?
Because it hurts being this good.

WHUPPA-WHUPPA-WHUPPA-
My turn to head out on a mission.

And I won't be returning empty-handed!

Just bandage-handed.

〈You're late!〉
〈Our apologies. We went to the wrong swamp.〉
〈No problem. What are we stealing this time?〉
〈A priceless painting. *Yellow Flowers.*〉
Translated from Japanese.

〈How long till we get there?〉
〈Two hours. Make yourself—〉

〈Comfortable.〉

The games.
BEEP!
BLOOP!
BRANG!

The socials.
_katana

The goat vids.
And finally...

The emails.

Dear Katana,
I come from Japan too, so we have one thing in common. But...maybe only one thing. Everyone says you're really edgy, and you get in trouble a lot. That sounds scary. I never get in trouble, but my classmates call me dull. I don't like that either! What's so bad about playing fair and square?

Sincerely,
Haru

Scary? Me?

ROOAR!

HAHA!
‹We have arrived.›

WHUPPA-WHUPPA-WHUPPA
Let me think on that and get back to you, Haru.
BLAZIN' THUMB!
Right now I've got a job to do—

And I need to jump right in!
*Honto?!
*Really?!
Billionaire's mansion. 
Nice place.
You can *sea* forever.

GRAB!
Flip-a-flip
I might as well get started.
It's gonna take those guys forever to find a parking spot.
A billion dollars buys a lot of security...
Fffut!
But not enough.
ZZZZ

fish-a-fish
ZZZZ

KEY CARD!

Move it along, Monopoly Man!

If I were a priceless painting, where would I hang out?
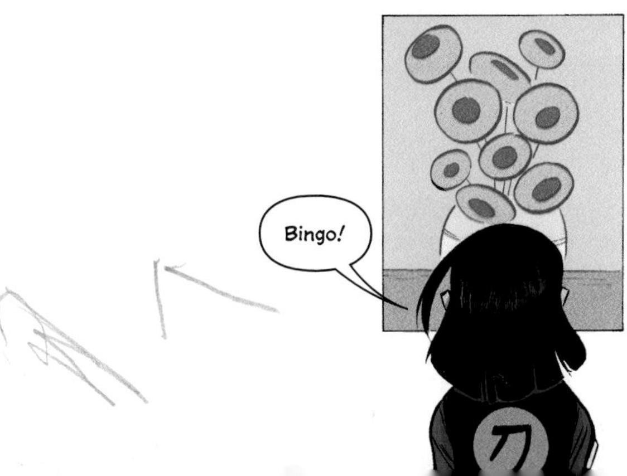
Bingo!

!!!

<Nice of you to join me. Better run!>

WHUPPA-WHUPPA-WHUPPA

<A pleasure doing business with you, boys.>

<Remember, we all get a cut. A deal is a deal.>
<I will contact our secret buyer and—>
<I've got a better idea...>

SHUCK!
SHUCK!

<Enjoy your cut, fellas.>
<I know I'll enjoy mine!>

SWOOOSH!!
Sayonara!

Nighttime at the Hall of Doom...
But midday in Tokyo.
WHUMP!
モンスター！
コ！&鳥
ビザロ

KLIK!

Dear Haru,

Perhaps we are not as different as you think. I too like to play fair and square. If I say everyone gets a cut, everyone does. I just like to get the nicest cut—that's just common sense!

(IT'S NOT!)

Your edgy bestie,
Katana

Fair and square...
And pretty!

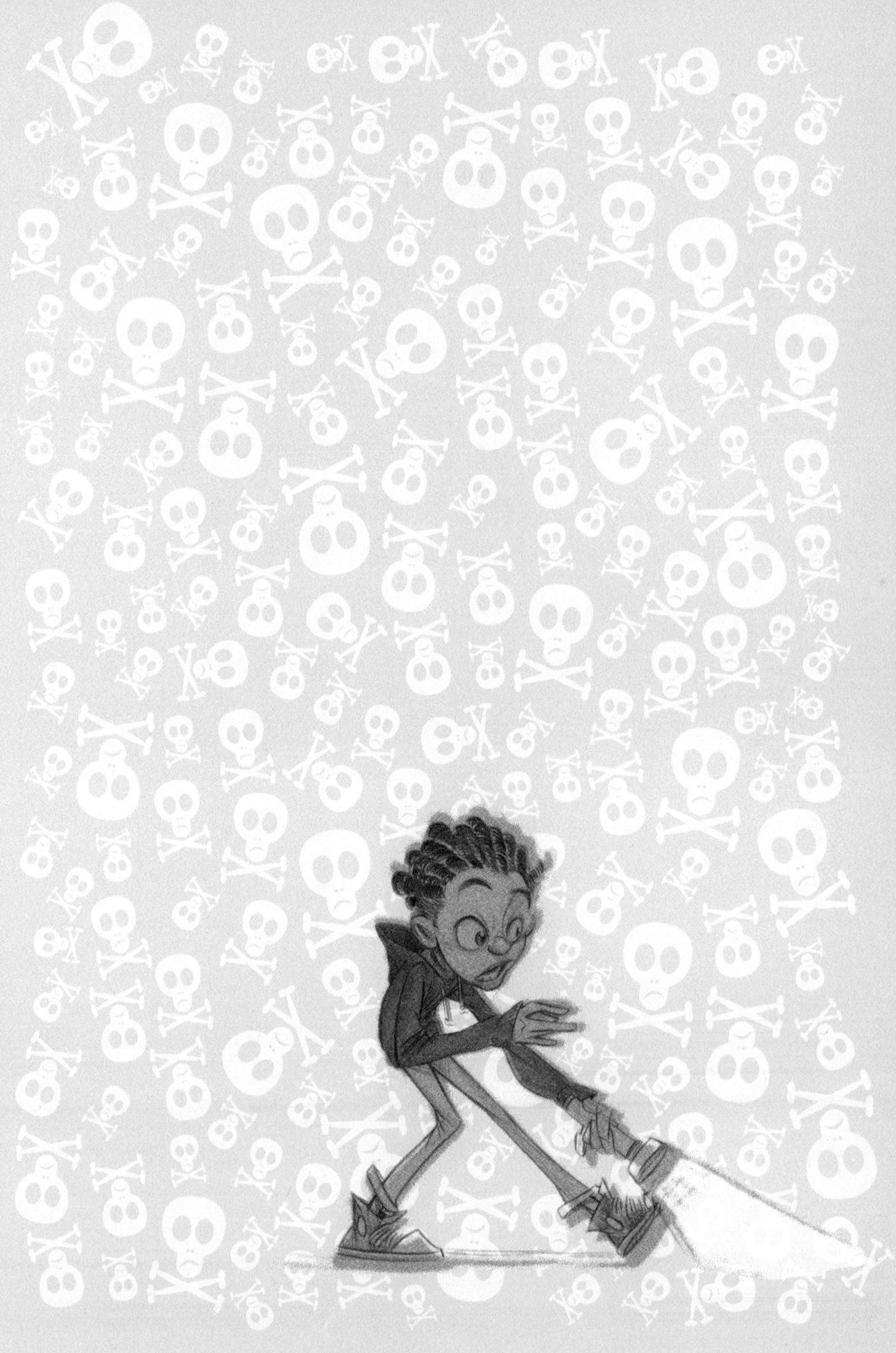

CHAPTER 8

Dear Black Manta

Sunrise outside
the Hall of Doom.
A new day dawns.
Nature awakes.
A sight glorious to behold.

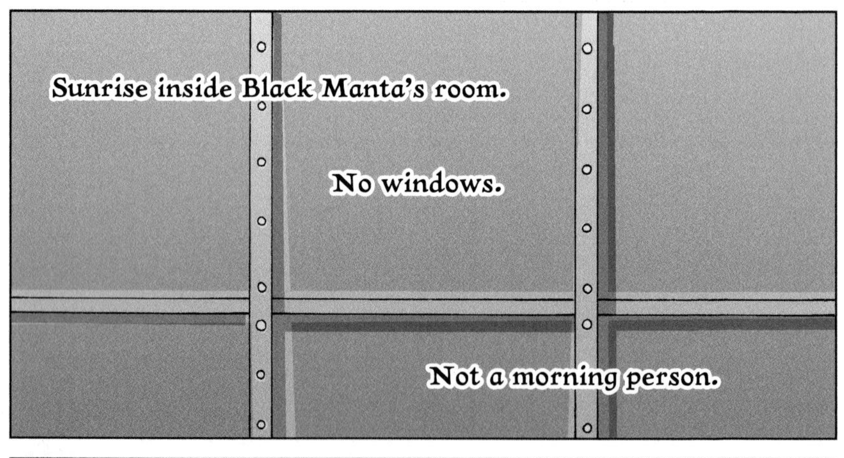
Sunrise inside Black Manta's room.
No windows.
Not a morning person.

He's only up because...
WORLD'S BEST PIRATE

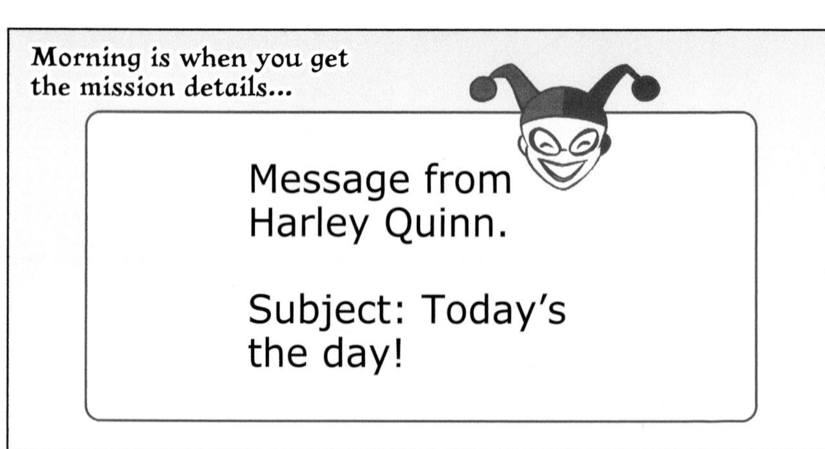
Morning is when you get the mission details...
Message from Harley Quinn.
Subject: Today's the day!

Today's the day! Make sure your weapons are charged and your underwear is clean. This is going to be a doozy!
Sluurrp!
WORLD'S BEST PIRATE

It's too early for a "doozy."
Maybe a donut...
CHARGING!

An email will wake me up.
This one's got an attachment.
Probably shouldn't click it. Could be a virus.

Or it *could* be a treasure map!
Ka-LICK!

Black Manta
Real name: David Hyde (shhh!)
Scourge of the high seas!
(And the low ones too!)
The world's most feared pirate,
Aquaman's greatest foe,
and my personal fave!
Good taste, kid.
This is my first email
to you so I guess I
should start it...
Dear Black Manta

My name is Artie Fishman, and I'm your biggest fan. My friends are like: Black Manta? Why not Aquaman? But I'm not into that do-gooder pretty boy.

The Piratical Adventures of Black Manta!
ARRRRR you READY?!
I tell them about the time you took every last piece of jewelry off that fancy cruise ship—and ate all the shrimp from the lunch buffet too!

Then I hit 'em with the time you dug up actual buried treasure in Tortuga!
By now, they're usually like: Aquaman who?
I usually finish up with the time you captured the king and queen of Herringland and had yourself named grand duke for life.
Everyone likes royal stories. It's like pirate Frozen.

Mmm. Good times...

I know everything about you—except what you're planning to do next! Come on, you can tell me. I'm Artie Fishman, your number one fan. And now all the other kids here are dying to know, too!

BLACK MANTA
MOST POPULAR
Finally!

But should I really tell some random kid my evil plans?

Of course!
He's my number one fan!

Well, actually, Artie, you're in luck. Me and the rest of the Legion of Doom are about to head out on a mission. It's top secret, of course, but just between us...
TAP TIP TAP

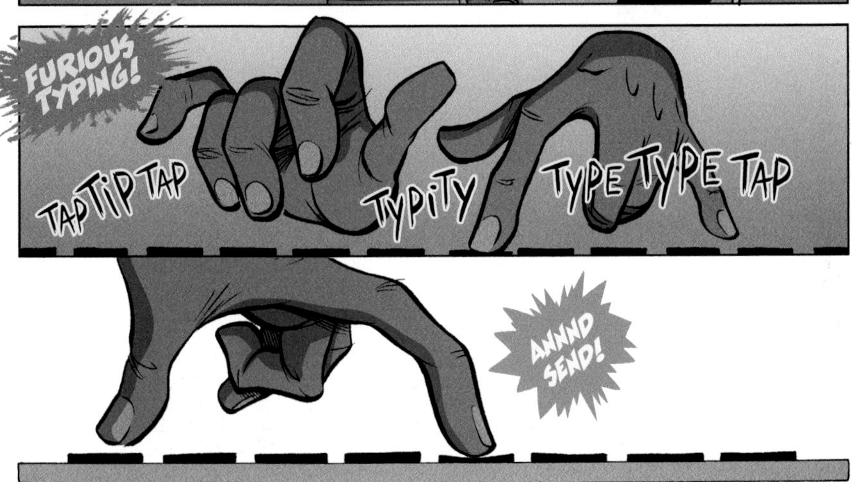
FURIOUS TYPING!
TAP TIP TAP
TYPITY
TYPE TYPE TAP
ANNND SEND!

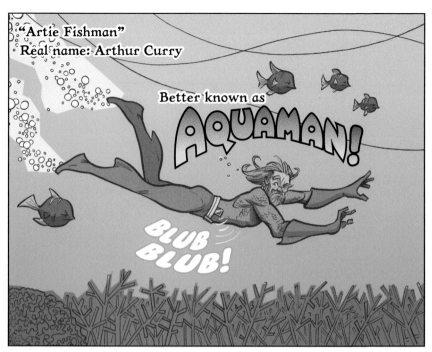

"Artie Fishman"
Real name: Arthur Curry

Better known as

AQUAMAN!

BLUB BLUB!

Waterproof case.
(Like, seriously waterproof.)

Message from Black Manta!

CHAPTER 9

DEAR DC SUPER-VILLAINS

Elsewhere in the seven seas, the mighty Manta Sub has embarked on another sinister mission.
Its cargo: the world's most notorious villains!
No doubt they are already planning fiendishly, plotting mercilessly...
HONK HONK!
And...arguing loudly?
My phone says to take a left at that reef-y thing.
Surface at once!
How can they fear our approach when they can't see us coming?
Will you all just SHUT UP?!
Grumble grumble
Soon, they reach their unsuspecting destination...
BLACKGATE PENITENTIARY!
Blurp!

The villains emerge into the salty air of Gotham Bay.
Where their "discussion" continues.

We're strong. We should bust down the front gate!

Sneaking in is the *purrfect* solution.

I say we swing in on ropes.

Let's examine the blueprints first.

This is why we gotta break Lex out of there.
None of us can agree on nothin'!

So how do we get in, smarty-shorts?
Squawk!

Compromise!
We sneak in the front gate on ropes, smash something, and grab the blueprints once we're inside!

I like it.

Wise.

Sensible.

What could go wrong?

And they're off!
UH-OH!
This was a horrible idea!
KA-BLOWW!
FRISH!
Yow! My furry butt!
SPLISH
Hiss! I hate water!
Sorry, guys!
Why couldn't I get the water cannon?

Luckily, I packed a backup plan.

CABLUMIUM!

SWISH!

KABLOOM!

Yattaaaa!

That knocked 'em on their guardrails!

STAMPEDE!

Uh-oh.

Aren't villains supposed to break **out** of prison?

Flick!

Yaah!

Grrr!

Good kitty! Don't eat me!

SHUMMP!

Puny human! You cannot resist my mind control!
Now tell me...

WHERE IS THE ONE KNOWN AS LUTHOR?

Maximum-security tower.
Top floor.

Follow me, villains. We have a towering task ahead!
Ooh, a tower. I feel like Rapunzel!

Knock, knock!

KRA-THOOM!

Doom's here!

Uh, halt?
Please?
HAHA
HA!

One little
guard...

How are you
going to stop
the Legion of
Doom?!

I guess
I'll just have
to...

Superman!

Green Lantern!

Cyborg!

Still Hawkgirl!

Batman!

The Flash!

Not Artie Fishman!

Wonder Woman!

I *hate* it when they do that!

Give it up, Legion.

You can't beat...
Usss...

Ooof!
Superman, what's wrong?!

A little present from Luthor's lab.
Superman's only weakness— Kryptonite.
Never leave home without it!
Stupor-man's lookin' a little green. *Hee hee!*

Fall back, Justice Leaguers! With Superman down, the Legion has the upper hand.

Can you fly?
Yes, I... I think so.
Then get to safety.
Everyone else, into the cell blocks!

PEW! PEW!
Fall back!

We need a plan, too.
We need to think this through careful—
GET 'EM!

TROMP! TROMP!
STOMP! STOMP!
Hey, watch where you're going, ya big ape!

We can cover more ground if we split up!

Remember, we're stronger if we stick together!
HA HA HA!

You're under my thumb now, Green Lantern.
Your green power ring can't beat my yellow energy!
Maybe not, Sinestro.

But there's thumb-thing you should know...
Oh yes? What's that?

KABLOAW!
Bump!

Help me, Katana!
I'll take this!
Sorry, Manta.
I feel like I'm stuck on the wrong team in dodgeball.

Let's get 'em, guys!

Uh, guys?
Uh-oh...

POW
POW
POW KAPOW!

SHE FITS, SHE SITS!
You know you're human like me, right?

Meanwhile, at the top of the tower...

Kind of loud out there today.

Maybe they're finally vacuuming...

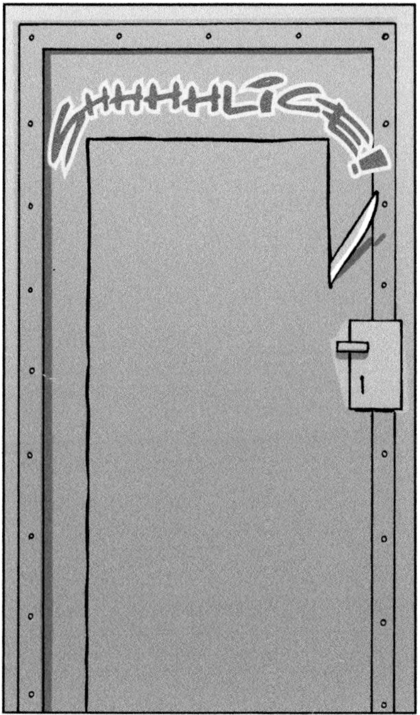

SHHHHLICE!

Katana?! Are you here to rescue me?
CHA-CLUNK!

Not anymore.
Good call.
You heroes really know how to make an entrance.

Sorry, Lex, but—
SHIIINK!

I've decided I'm not cut out for this villain thing!

I'm a hero n—
OW!
KIK!

Whoa!
Oof!
KRONK!
TOPPLE!

Gross! I just bounced off an *eyeball.*
It was no picnic for me, either.

Oh, great. Now I freed the Joker.
Smooth hero-ing.
HA HA!
JK1977

I don't understand it.
With my Kryptonite, the Legion had more than enough muscle to beat the Justice League.
Maybe so, Luthor.
But all the power in the world means nothing unless you work—

TOGETHER!

Don't worry.

I'll mail it for you.

Because you're not going anywhere!

LL1979

Due to the sudden demand for reinforced cells, the villains are forced into a horrible fate...

GG1959
Roommates.
BRUSH-A-BRUSH
Must you paint so *loudly?*
I feel like a caged tiger in here!
Please tell me this large box of sand is not what I think it is...

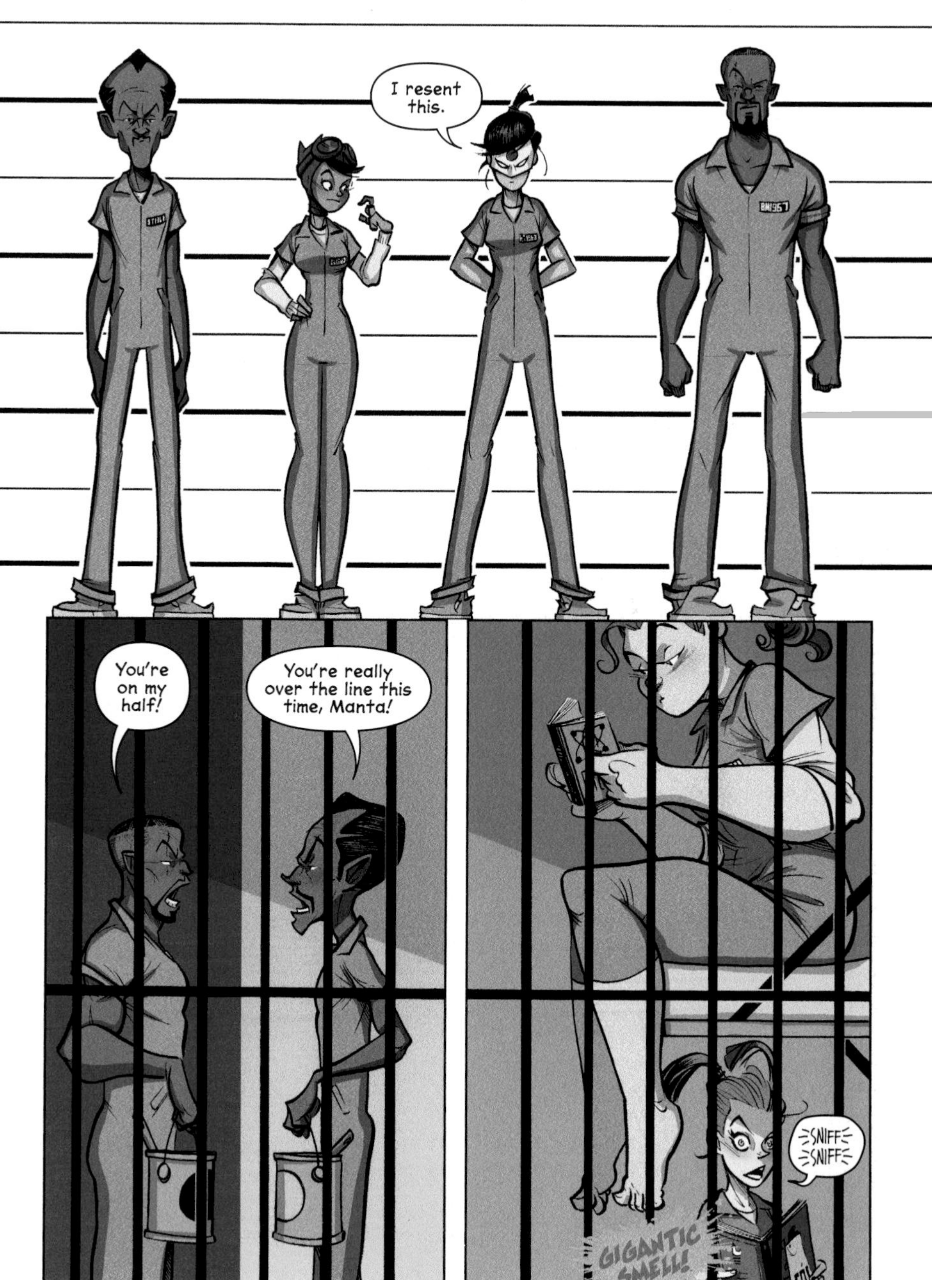
I resent this.
You're on my half!
You're really over the line this time, Manta!
SNIFF SNIFF
GIGANTIC SMELL!

Perfect.

Now, where should I hang it?

GG1959

Oh, I know!

grumble

It's going to be a long 87 years.

Meanwhile, on the interwebs...

From: The Legion of Doom Tip Line of Evil

Letters wanted. Send care of Blackgate Penitentiary.

We're pretty bored in here.

Sincerely,
The Legion of Doom

WHO'S WHO IN THE LEGION OF DOOM

LEX LUTHOR

Secret identity: Nope. Villainy like this must shine.

Villainous abilities: A super-genius, constant plotter, and ingenious inventor with endless wealth and resources.

Weakness: Can't stop fighting Superman—the one man he can't beat!

HARLEY QUINN

(Not-so) secret identity: Dr. Harleen Quinzel

Villainous abilities: She's strong, agile, smart, and totally unpredictable in battle—a real heavy hitter (with a real heavy hammer)!

Weaknesses: Impulsive, reckless, and rash. When you cause this much trouble, you're gonna cause some for yourself.

CATWOMAN

Secret identity: Selina Kyle

Villainous abilities: Sneaky, agile, and packing some very sharp claws.

Weakness: Cat naps.

KATANA

Secret identity: Tatsu Yamashiro

Villainous abilities: Swift, strong, skilled...Is she the best martial artist in the world? Sword of!

Weaknesses: Dropped swords and two-day-old sushi.

BLACK MANTA

Secret identity: David Hyde

Villainous abilities: A swashbuckling pirate in a high-tech armored suit of his own design (yeah, he's that smart). Enhanced strength, energy blasts, and super-swimming.

Weaknesses: Pillage-prone. Driven to distraction by Aquaman.

SINESTRO

Secret identity: Thaal Sinestro

Villainous abilities: Energy blasts, force fields, flight, and the ability to create objects out of "hard light"—all thanks to his power ring.

Weaknesses: Angry, proud, controlling—that's Thaal, folks.

GORILLA GRODD

Secret identity: A mild-mannered monkey named Mr. Bumbles. Just kidding. None.

Villainous abilities: Super-strength and agility. Mind control, telekinesis, telepathy.

Weakness: Doesn't wear pants.

GIGANTA

Secret identity: Doris Zuel

Villainous abilities: Can grow to giant size—and strength!

Weakness: Bumps her head a lot.

AUXILIARY MEMBERS!

These guys seem too nice!

PHOTO BY FRANCINE DAVETA

MICHAEL NORTHROP

Writer of *Dear DC Super-Villains*

Villainous abilities: Gets characters into all kinds of trouble. Creates extreme amounts of work for artist. Punishing puns.

Weaknesses: Gummy bears. Extreme resistance to exercise. The opposite of super-agility.

Michael Northrop is the *New York Times* bestselling author of 14 books for kids and teens. His first young adult novel, *Gentlemen*, earned him a Publishers Weekly Flying Start citation, and his second, *Trapped*, was an Indie Next List selection. His first middle grade novel, *Plunked*, was named one of the best children's books of the year by the New York Public Library and was selected for NPR's Backseat Book Club. He is originally from Salisbury, Connecticut, a small town in the foothills of the Berkshire mountains, where he mastered the arts of BB gun shooting, tree climbing, and field goal kicking with only moderate injuries. After graduating from NYU, he worked at *Sports Illustrated for Kids* magazine for 12 years, the last five of those as baseball editor.

PHOTO BY JOSI VICENTIN

GUSTAVO DUARTE

Artist of *Dear DC Super-Villains*

Villainous abilities: Turning ink into evildoers! Filling pages with an impending sense of doom. Humor that will make you laugh so hard it hurts.

Weaknesses: Inability to wake up early. Total immunity to alarm clocks. Warning: May turn into zombie.

Gustavo Duarte is a Brazilian cartoonist, graphic designer, and comics creator who currently resides in São Paulo. For the last 20 years, Duarte's cartoons and illustrations have been published in some of the most popular publications in Brazil. In 2009, Duarte began publishing his own comics like *Monsters!*, *Có!*, *Birds*, and others. In addition to his own works, Duarte has also written and illustrated comics for major publishers including DC (*Bizarro*) and Marvel (*Guardians of the Galaxy* and *Lockjaw*), among others.

The author of *CatStronauts*, Drew Brockington, welcomes you to *Metropolis Grove*, the suburb where no kid believes in Superman—he's a big-city myth, they're sure of it.

But newcomer Sonia Patel still believes! And when she goes exploring with her new neighbors, they find a cave full of Super-memorabilia that launches them into a *bizarre* adventure with the most unlikely of heroes!

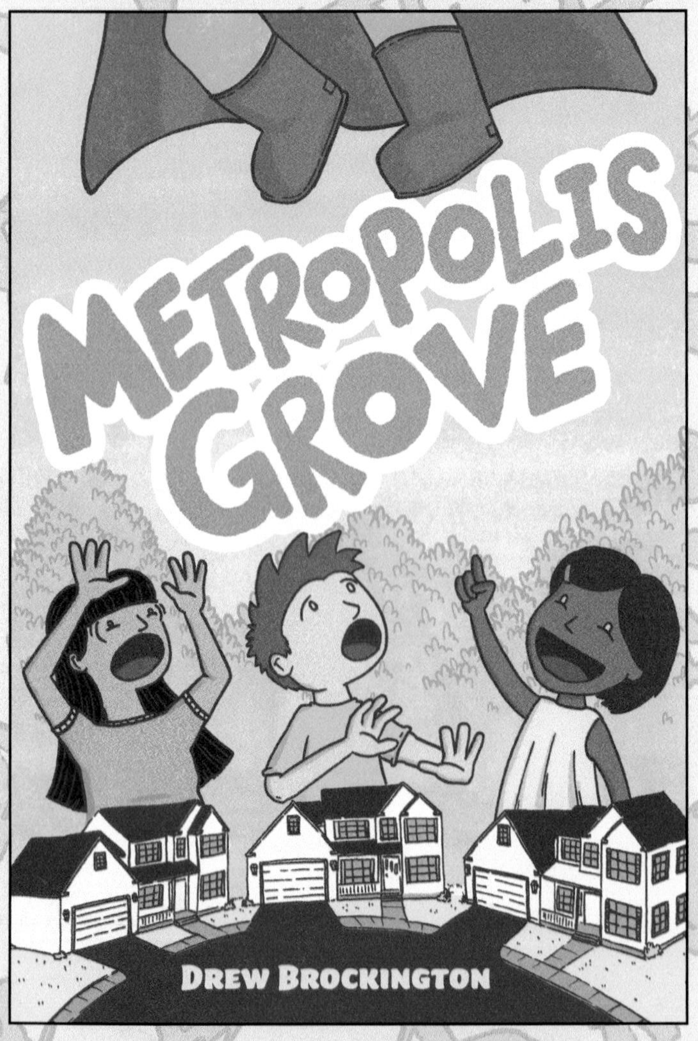

Keep reading for a special sneak peek of *Metropolis Grove*—available May 2021!

M.G.

SLAM!
Morning, Duncan!
MORFWIN!

What was that?
Sorry. Waffle.
Morning, Alex. Are you ready to do this?

Yes! So excited.
I've got everything: rope, nails, my dad's drill, and about five rolls of duck tape.
Rad. That drill will be handy.

I figure we can make our way to the creek and scout out a spot for building the fort around there.
THE GLADE
I know a place! Maybe we can even—
DUNCAN!

I want you back by dinnertime.
Okay, Mom.

I LOVE YOU!
Why does she always say that in front of my friends...

He He He He He He He He

I LOVE YOU TOO!

Okay, where were we?
Maybe we can find that old abandoned boat, too?
It could have some cool supplies for the fort on it.
TAP
Yeah! Good thinking!
This is the perfect way to start off summer vacation!
It's going to be so fun!
SOLD
HONK
SOLD
SUPERMOVER
SUPERMOVER

Hey, someone is finally moving into that house.
That SOLD sign has been up forever.
SUPERMOVER
SUPERMOVER
SOLD

SCHOOOOM!
Do you think the new owners will have kids?
I would *LOVE* that.

Don't get me wrong, we're BFFs forever...
But it would be nice to have another kid on the block.

Okay. Moment of truth.
The car doors are opening!

That's not a kid.

Nope.

Definitely not a kid.

JACKPOT!

Hi, I'm Alex.
I'm Duncan.
Hiya! I'm Sonia.

We just moved here from Metropolis!
Do you live in the neighborhood?
Can we be best friends?!
SU

Uhh...we kinda are the neighborhood.
Yeah, we're the only two kids on this block.

Well, now there are three kids on this block.

I'd invite you in to hang out at my house, but we're a little busy at the moment.
SUPERMOVER
FOR SALE
SOLD

We were just about to go play in the woods.
Yeah, we're going to build a huge fort.
Do you want to come with us?

Really?! You want me to come?

I do! I do! I want to go!
I just need to ask my parents first.

MOM, DAD! CAN I GO PLAY IN THE WOODS WITH MY NEW NEIGHBORHOOD FRIENDS?!

Please?
Yes, Sonia, you may go.

Stick close to your new friends.
I don't want you getting lost on our first day at our new home.
CLAP
CLAP
CLAPPY

All right! Let's build that fort!

Come on, new best friends! Into the woods!
MARCH MARCH MARCH
Uh, Sonia?

Yeah?
The woods are this way.

I knew that.

WOW! This place got wild fast.

Is it safe to walk back here?
It's pretty safe.

Just watch out for tree roots and snakes.

He's kidding about the snakes.

You haven't been around nature very much, have you, Sonia?
I mean... I go to Centennial Park a lot in Metropolis. But it's nothing like this.

I've been a city kid my whole life, I guess.
Wait. You mean you've ***never*** been out of the city?

I went to Central City last year for one of my dad's work conferences.
Does that count?
Not really. You went from one city to another.

Oh.
It's not a bad thing! You just don't have any experience.
Fortunately for you, Alex and I have experience up to our ears.
Yeah! We can teach you everything about the woods!

How much longer is it?
Almost there...

I think...

Are we lost?

According to our heading...
THE GLADE

It should be just up ahead.

Sonia's new friends introduce her to life in a small town—you can join their adventures in May 2021 when METROPOLIS GROVE is in stores!